The Onyx Coronet

Leilani Graceffa

First paperback edition May 2020

Book cover design by Leilani Graceffa

ISBN 978-1-7350952-0-2 (Paperback)
ISBN 978-1-7350952-1-9 (Hardcover)
ISBN 978-1-7350952-2-6 (Ebook)

For more information, visit www.leilanigraceffa.com.

Refuse to give in to the clouds overcasting, someone will understand. For Christina, all of the smiles that succumbed, and whom this may concern.

Chapitre 1

Ever since a gloomy cloud developed over my head, I am sure she swore to herself, she would stay away from me for as long as she is alive. Even when she inherits her mother's throne, I have no chance. Princess Maxine. Once and to this day, the beauteous love of my life, and perchance, my future princess. But she scorns me because of what I have done to her and many other heirs as children.

'Perchance? I am the immortal Prince Zane of Emberbourne, and she will be mine!'

There it is, the malicious shadow side of me that I refuse to be fond of, the part of me that draws everybody away. I am different from the rest now. I was once courteous and timid until I was wittingly cursed by a voodoo conjurer while roaming in a coppice nearby my kingdom as a little boy. But they do not know that. I do not think they would consider it. It is easier for them to conclude that I have let the prestige and my conceit get to my head. Regard me or not, it is far from the verity.

I wish she would listen to me and come to understand that. She leaves the entire chamber silent, lucidly bitter and infuriated with her mother and father, "I REFUSE TO MARRY SOMEONE AS VAIN AND INSOLENT AS ZANE!"

As much as I have been longing to have her in my arms finally and show her that I am well from how this hex makes me out to be, her stubbornness is immense, almost enticing. She would not even look at me if I were to address her.

'She better look at me when I am talking to her. I am not reluctant to use my sorcery to bewitch a princess.'

No, no, please do not. I can talk to her if she lets me. "Maxine!" I call, chasing after her. "Do not roam off, princess! Where are you going?"

"Away from you!"

Ever since I did something neither her nor any of the other heirs will acquit me for, she has been very testy with nobody else but me. I put one of the heirs, also Maxine's best friend, Prince Nathaniel, under a hasty ageing curse, with no knowledge of how to evert it.

She and my dear and only friend Princess Charlotte witnessed me curse him, but they did not tell the mistress or any authority. Now while Nathaniel still lies dying as the clock ticks, with no antidote, I am still here trying to keep my mystic secret at bay. As much as I yearn to express remorse for doing such a thing to my kind, I am unable to, not willfully.

'But I am not going to find an antidote, am I? I cannot forget that he is the reason I cannot have Maxine. I hope he perishes! She can choose to discard me, but she will regret it, right now! If I cannot have her, nobody can!' I raise one of my arms, aiming at her back, I cast out something shadowy from my finger, that pierces her spine and causes her to fall onto her knees.

"Maxine!" Look what you have done now!

*'She deserves it, '*My shadow behalf demands, *'leave the woman to suffer!'*

"I am not going to do that..." I murmur to him or myself. I disdain his blunt demands to me, regarding all the menials looking over the railings to glimpse what just befell. "Damn it..." I scoop up her benumbed body, then begin to use my smoke speed to leave the grounds as fast as the light of a diminishing ember. I hope I did not use the same spell that I used on Nathaniel. "Max!" I call out as she lies tranced in my arms, her eyes starting to roll into the back of her head. I know who could fix this, a witch doctor. I have had only one experience with one before, trying to rid myself of my powers and my shadow that came with them. The method she used only strengthened them.

But if they are taking care of Nathaniel and giving their all to keep that spell I cast tamed, they can and will undoubtedly heal Maxine. "Pardon me, love," I say to a woman with long, copper-coloured dreads past her shoulders, carrying a large pail of what seems to be herbs and plants in her hands. She turns around, noticing the unresponsive princess in my arms. She knows who I need. Without a word, she gestures for me to follow her.

As I am keeping up with this woman, the entire tribe seems to have their eyes on me, possibly curious as to why I am carrying someone who looks similar to them. Maybe they can sense the energy I discharge, or they are quietly despising me, as they do with the rest of the royals, as we have learned.

'Oh, come on! You are doing all of this for a frail girl!'

I would demand him to shut his damn trap and let me breathe for once, but I would look foolish, demanding myself, with all of these people having their eyes on me.

"Agatha," She says with a thick cadence, assuring this witch doctor that she has a visitor.

"I knew it was you, Zane..." This middle-aged woman appears eerie to me. Her face painted with white dots just beneath her icy blue eyes, and grey streaks already conjoining the red hair that suits her dark skin. Distinctive plants, candles, and coloured glass bottles organized but everywhere. Her energy intimidates me.

'You should have left her where she was, you caitiff! What are you going to tell her parents?'

That is, for once, a good one, what am I going to tell them? "You tell them, you did that, this is your fault!"

'My pleasure... move aside, you milksop!' He cackles.

I hate sharing a body with this fopdoodle. "And do not be a prick!"

"Ah, your highness! I have been looking for you everywhere." I say as I stride into the chamber. "Your daughter... she is not feeling well..."

"Maxine?" Her mother asks, "What is wrong with her? Is she all right?"

"I do not know. She might have gone to her bedchamber to rest."

'Is that all you can do?'

"Quiet..." I whisper to myself as I go to sit into my seat, awaiting my plot to fall into place. Catherine, her mother, promptly asks one of their menials to check on the princess. Good luck with that. Hereafter, the woman returns, then whispers into the queen's ear. The white-faced expression of fear that overcomes her face after doing so leaves everyone else quietly perturbed.

"THEY LOST OUR DAUGHTER?!"

"I am afraid so, your highness."

"DO NOT JUST STAND THERE! INFORM THE CAVALRY!"

I have never fathomed her potential of getting angry. She is usually a reserved woman. However, not at this moment, and she will not be for a good while.

'This is vile! Just tell her where Maxine is!'

"Shut up..."

'Let me out!' *He demands, attempting to jostle me for his place.*

"You wanted me to do this..." I growl.

'NOT LIKE THIS! MOVE!'

To prevent appearing foolish and eccentric faintly talking and arguing with myself since the coward will not let up, I get up and damn near mindlessly leave the chamber. "Sit down! You wanted me to do this, and I am going to do it my way!"

'What is the rest of your plan?'

"They know not to go near those tribe villages; they believe most of them are evil, as they were taught. They will not find her if one has her. Get a grip. You will be able to get the princess and bring her back while they are still looking for her."

'But what if...'

"There is no "what if," you pansy. We are on a time limit, and I need your complete trust, or this will not work. Do you want me to help you or not?"

'Yes.'

I need to figure out how to use and control my powers... and him. However, I am not sure whom to go to for it. I cannot go to the woman who cursed me; I do not know who she is. I do not think anybody does.

I hold sheer malignity towards her for this, and if I ever get to be face-to-face with her, I will cast the same spell I... well, my shadow side, put on Prince Nathaniel, on her. See how she likes having an irrevocable spell cast onto her and having to suffer due to it.

'Oh, shut it! I am not that bad. After all, I am still helping you from getting chastised after hurting the princess.'

"You did that."

'I know I did, and it was damn savoury to see her like that! So, unless my help does not gratify you, I advise you to accept that chaos and pain turn me on, I am an important part of you, your shadow aspect. Keep your degrading thoughts about me to yourself.'

"You are sick," I mumble before taking off my crown.

'What are you doing? Sometime later, you are going to have to get the girl and return her.'

"Yeah, I know." I have never felt this drained.

'Or are you just broken-hearted?'

"Shut up." I try not to mind him and his replies to me and my thoughts. I do not think I will wear my crown tonight; in case I get caught or recognized. I can always summon it when I need it.

"Zane?"

"Yes, mother?" I answer as I turn towards her.

"Are you okay, love?" She asks with a soft tone, before extending her arms out for a hug. "I am sorry..."

"She never liked me anyway." She once did, as a friend. But those days are long gone. Although I have known the entire time, it still feels like a spearhead is piercing my heart... hence the tears welling my eyes. She will never understand. I embrace my mother but drop my head into her shoulder.

'Oh, suck it up, you damn milksop!'

Standing in front of a window I opened, I ask myself before sliding my hood over my head, "What is the rest of the plan again?"

'Just get the girl and return her to her room before you get caught.'

Easier said than done. I use my smoke speed from the window to arrive at the tribal village as fast as I could, with the partial energy my body has stored from a quick nap I took proceeding to drain. Again. I have to do this quick before I run out of energy and my shadow side comes out with his own.

Now the yard or garden of this village is lit by erected torches. But it does not look like anyone is out, as they were earlier today, anymore. I think I may remember the way back to where the witch doctor made me leave Maxine.

'You think you may remember? You better remember it! If your energy drains, I am not carrying her or your ass back to your bedchamber.'

That is nice to know. He never wants to help. I am running this time, since the more I use my powers, the quicker my energy will drain. But I could... use my profound senses. I get onto my knees, then put my ear close to the gravel below. Footsteps, I hear light footsteps, but in a couple of paces. A couple of people are still up and about. "Show me a path." Starting at my feet, the gravel beneath me illuminates, leading to two separate paths ahead of me. I quickly choose a path to follow. Furthermore, as quickly as I begin to follow the path, I notice the second one, at one point, traverses this one.

This mazed path leads me to someone walking with their back to me. By their small appearing figure, I assume it to be a woman, holding a small lantern and with a hood over her head, right ahead of me. However, as I am nearing approaching this person, the other path suddenly switches to traversing at this point, as if the other person is trying to find their way around as well. "Hey!" I call out to the person ahead, just before this second person darts across their path like they are being hunted down by someone or something. Maxine. She is running from me. "Max!" I use my smoke speed to catch her in an instant.

"LET ME GO!" She screams as she struggles to withstand my hold on her. "HELP!"

'Shut the little girl up! I am trying to sleep!'

"Relax!" I claim. "I am going to take you back home, Max."

She snarls at me. "NO! I do not need your help, Zane!"

"I know the way back to your kingdom."

"I do not care!" She growls, breaking free as I loosen my grip on her. I will not let her go out there by herself. "Are you sure?" I ask,

11

bracing almost the rest my energy to paralyze her body. She does not answer. I seize her movement clutching onto the sides of her body, then I squeeze some of my energy into her, just as she turns her back to me. Letting her now, once again, benumbed body, collapse into my arms. Do not worry; she will wake in a few hours.

'Ah, so you have learned something from me. Well done.'

I roll my eyes, "Yeah, sure." Carrying her body, I use my speed the whole way to her kingdom, Hazelfell, where I put her into her bed. But before I leap out the window, avoiding being caught by a menial or knight, I plant a kiss on her forehead. I know she would choke me out for that... if she ever finds out, I kissed her.

'Clever.'

With my energy on the verge of being completely drained, I finally return to my bedchamber. Where I do not notice a bird, a hawk, perched on the canopy of my bed until I close my window. It is Princess Charlotte's tamed hawk, Melia, holding a small note between her large talons. "Come here, Melia," I say as I extend my arm out towards her. Not wanting to pierce my skin with her talons, she lands onto my shoulder instead, and I steal the note from them. I read the small handwriting:

[I saw you. See me tomorrow.

Charlotte].

Chapitre 2

I knew someone would recognize me last night, even when I tried to be as obscured as I could. But at least it was Charlotte. So, now I am almost at her kingdom, Basinhurst, to return her hawk and see her. "Go get her, Melia," I say before letting her fly from my shoulder, up and into Charlotte's room.

A couple of hands grab onto the outer sill of the window, then long fiery red hair appears. "Come in!" She calls, giving me a huge grin.

When she turns her attention from me, I fly up to her window. I scare her, just as I expect me appearing at her window so suddenly would.

"Oh!" She jumps, "Damn it, Zane! Are you... floating?"

I shrug, "Sort of."

"Okay, that is nice... come in."

"What is up?"

"Your powers. Have you tried to get rid of them?"

'Damn, she is good.'

I freeze at the mention of them. "I... I have tried with a witch doctor once. They got worse..." Even though she witnessed me cast that curse on Nathaniel, I am not sure how she knows I really have powers. I have not shown her, or she has not seen any more than that.

"I know about your powers, Zane. I know you have not seen me since that incident with Nathaniel; I was not avoiding you. I have been studying the entire time; I knew something was up with you. I have been training with a witch doctor, and she told me you were cursed."

"I was cursed." I never thought she cared to know. "I did not think you cared to know what is going on with me. Thank you, Charlotte."

"Not a problem." She smiles, "I am sorry it seemed like I was avoiding you all that time. I let my teacher use a spell on me, I am not sure how she is going to undo it, but I have powers now."

"You what?" My eyes widen. "Charlotte, it is permanent! Once you get cursed, it stays with you."

"Not if your teacher knows how to undo it. In your case, it is, since you most likely do not know who cast the spell on you."

Sadly. "Is it possible for me to learn from this witch doctor as well? I am almost clueless about how to control my powers, and..."

'You better not say it, if you mention me... shut your trap!'

"Other things..."

'That is what I thought.'

She quickly purses her lips. "I suppose I could... but I have books that I found that could help you. We can try those first." She pulls out something, a large basket, from underneath her bed, and we begin our quest to learn about our own, as well as each other's powers.

I remember being the kid I was, playing and having fun with the other kids before this curse mess. That is how it feels being with Charlotte now, except we are not kids playing, we are using magic. In a concealed field not far from her kingdom, we emulously, but carefully, cast spells at each other and compose things using our energies.

It is helping me control my powers and learn more about them. The only thing I still cannot control is my shadow, and I guess I will eventually have to tell her about him if I want complete control of them.

"ZANE!" I hear Charlotte cry out as a weird ball of hazy light comes hurtling towards me, "WATCH OUT!"

The light clashes with my body before I can make it backfire, knocking me from where I am standing, far back into the trunk of a tree.

"Are you okay?!"

I barely hear her voice ask from afar, but not because whatever she cast nearly knocked me cold. 'No, no! You better not!' I yell at my shadow, who has now overtaken my body with a malicious intention. 'LET IT GO! She did not mean that!'

"YOU ARE NOT GOING TO TAKE THAT FROM A FRAIL PRINCESS!" I make sure to choose one of my most caustic spells. "Fighting me will only make it worse for her!" Waiting for a reply to her question, she instantly notices a shift in the energy expending around me, the scowl on my face, and the energy garnering in one of my hands.

'NO!'

I hurl the growing ball of energy at her, which causes her body to fling back some amount of feet from where she stood. I wait for a few seconds to see whether she would quickly recover and get back up from it.

'WHAT DID YOU DO?!'

"SHUT IT! She deserved it!" She stays down for a little too long. As I begin to walk over to where her body hit the ground, not that I care whether she is injured or not, I hear laughter. When I get to her, I peer over her body, ready to impose another cold spell on her. But instead, a light strikes me, forcing me to tumble, then fall back.

"What was that?" I hear her chuckle over me before I open my eyes. "That was not you, Zane."

"My shadow side," I answer as I stand up, "he usually comes out when he is angry. I cannot control him."

"Sounds more like a demon. When did you get that?"

'She must want more of what I just gave her! Shut this bitch up!'

"He came with my powers. He cursed Nathaniel."

"So... that was not your fault?"

"It was," I say, "jealousy. I was jealous. I like Maxine, and Nathaniel is her best friend. I knew she would choose him over me, and I thought I could control that. Even though I did not willfully make him come out to curse him, I knew my jealousy would bring him out." I did like her. There is no point in trying when she hates me with a burning passion.

Charlotte suddenly stops talking and turns her head, staring at something far away, behind me. It seems to have grabbed her outright attention. Curious of what she is looking at, I turn my head to see a small, decrepit appearing figure walking away from us.

"Who?" I ask.

"I do not know... but nobody else should know about this part of the forest." Questioning whether this odd person would reveal themselves or continue with wherever they are heading, Charlotte hesitantly calls after them. "HEY!"

'It is her...'

"Who? Give us more than that, please."

'Philantha. She forced me to be stuck with you, dimwit!'

"Charlotte!" I dive forward onto her, causing both of us to fall into the tall grass. "Wh–" is all that can escape her mouth before I cover her mouth. The woman slowly turns her head towards us before fully turning around.

"You are crushing me, Zane..." Charlotte whispers.

"I am sorry." Just as I believe the tall grass is almost wholly cloaking us from where she is standing, my eyes make direct contact with her gold eyes. She has the small figure of an older woman, but she does not facially appear to be old. But aside from that, her energy is perilous. "Was she watching us?"

'Yes.'

"You knew?" He refrains from answering my question, which undoubtedly means yes. She sees me, but she does not walk towards us. She just gives a sly smile, turns back around, and proceeds on her way. I keep Charlotte down until this woman eventually disappears into the haze of green. "You are telling me you knew who the bitch was all these years?!" I bark.

Charlotte cocks her head questioningly after brushing off her dress, "Who are you talking to?"

"My shadow side! He will not answer me!"

"Whoa, whoa, Zane. Calm down," She says, "what is wrong?"

"That was her! That was the woman who cursed me! She was watching us!"

"How do you know?"

"He just told me!"

"Okay. Do not freak out... since you know now, we could just try to find her and let her undo the spell."

I do not think she would be courteous enough even to do so. That depraved look she had in her eyes when we made eye contact, and her energy... she is not amicable. "I guess. But if she turns us into sacks of stacked cattle, do not say we did not get warned."

I cannot be angry when my shadow has been against me and degrading me every chance he gets since I have first perceived him. I just cannot fathom that he has been keeping this information from me. Knowing I have been longing to get rid of what has been destroying me and hurting the people around me for far too long. Now he will not tell me anything. He knows he slipped up.

"Maybe she will know about her. Follow me." Charlotte answers before suddenly altering into a beaming mist and speeding ahead of me.

Damn. She did not tell me she had speed as well. I quickly follow after her. She was telling me about the witch doctor who has been training her, Agatha. Surprisingly, the same woman I left Maxine with. She probably already knows about me from Charlotte. When we arrive in the village, Charlotte immediately takes me to Agatha. She recognizes me, and we hastily begin to explain everything that just happened to her. "She appeared old from behind, and she was wearing a hood, I could not see her face. When I did see it, she looked like she was my mother's age. She looked directly at me and gave me this sinister look... and she had these weird gold eyes."

"She sounds like a shapeshifter. Tell me more." She responds after listening. "Is it possible that you know her name?"

"I think it is... Pil... Philan..." I stutter. "Something demented!"

"Philantha!"

"Yes! Thank you!"

"We have heard of her. She is a virulent woman. She got exiled from the Zoneian tribe, miles from here."

"Is there any way I could get her to undo this curse?"

"I am afraid I do not know the answer to that. Philantha is not a witch doctor, shaman, or a healer in any kind of way. She is a vicious voodoo priestess, and I cannot teach you much about voodoo or its contents."

I sigh. "Unfortunately."

"There is one thing you can try, but Charlotte now has that power. You will need her for it."

"What is it?" I ask solemnly.

She stays sitting in her place for about a minute, thinking, until she gets up and walks to the other side of the room to grab something... a light blue liquid in a small, corked glass elixir bottle. "This is all I can think of. It only works with weapons like swords and archery, so use it wisely."

"Hmm..." Charlotte murmurs, "what does it do?"

"It is a drainer. It should be able to weaken her powers or maybe even deprive her completely of them since she is an opposer. You need to find a way to get this inside of her. However, I cannot guarantee it will overpower her."

"We will take it."

"We forgot to ask her how we would be able to find Philantha since she is a shapeshifter."

Charlotte purses her lips for a second. "But she does not know we are looking for her. So, she most likely still looks the same. We can just ask around, giving her physical description."

"That is true."

I stand up. "When are we going to start looking?"

"Hopefully, tomorrow. Our energies are on the verge of draining, after today."

"You are always right." I smile. "See you tomorrow."

"See you." She replies, already sounding weary.

I may not have my crush or most of the other princes and princesses, but at least I still have Charlotte on my side. She is one of the most loyal people anyone could ask for.

As I am heading back to my kingdom, I look at the lush field below for a moment, and it appears vacant as it usually is... for a second. Until something dark moving, more like tearing through the tall grass, grabs my attention. "No..." I whisper to myself, "is it... her?"

'Yes, it is.'

"Oh, so now you want to talk and answer me. Where have you been?"

'Go fuck yourself.'

"You go do that yourself, you are the narcissistic version of me, after all. Moreover, you waited so long to tell me something I have wanted to know since I got stuck with you."

'I am not listening...'

I roll my eyes. "That is all you are good at doing anyway." I stay elevated, trailing her with my eyes as she trots across the land. Where is she headed? I keep myself in my smoke form as I begin to follow her from afar. Hopefully, she cannot sense my energy from here. She still appears as how we last saw her, small figure and weak locks of black hair with grey streaks.

When I follow her long enough, she unknowingly leads me to a small, castle-like structure beneath a canopy of soaring trees, almost miles from the forest. I do not think it is visible from above. It might be where she stays. If so, she has people we will probably have to get through first. Hence all of the people, mainly knights and monks I see, wearing armour with weapons and riding horses in a field just nearby.

Chapitre 3

A s I watch Charlotte climb down the large stones from her room window, wearing heavy full plate armour with a scabbard, I ask, "What are we using?"

"This sword. I could not find any bow and arrows, and do not want to risk a crossbow."

"Okay. Are you sure you want to wear all of that during this?"

"What are you trying to imply? Of course."

"I know it is heavy on you."

"It is not heavy. It was customized to fit my size." She frowns, "You wear yours every day. Is all of that heavy on you?"

'Damn,' He laughs brazenly, 'you better shut up!'

"Ouch, I am sorry. Just making sure."

She raises her eyebrows at me. "Where do we look first?"

"We do not have to look," I affirm, "I followed her yesterday. She went into some structure miles from here."

"You are still here and did not get turned into stacked cattle, so I assume you did not get caught, or she could not see you." She laughs.

"I stayed far back, so both." We begin our brief journey to our destination, fleeting past all the trees through the forest for miles. If those knights and monks do not have powers themselves, then we together should have a definite advantage against them, no matter the number of them. When we arrive, we stand on a high, outstretched tree branch, hoods over our heads and concealed by surrounding leaves and more nature. They are not able to see us, but we can see most of them. "Ready?"

"Yes."

I forge a bow and arrows with my energy, aim, then start to launch multiple arrows at some of the knights and monks ahead. We patiently watch as they begin to scramble around each other for cover. "Let's go!" We charge into the field together, enchanting and taking on any and everybody who finds our duo combative. However, it does not stay an easy battle; they start coming at us with arrows and crossbows, and an arrow nearly strikes me. Charlotte and I retreat to each other, backs against each other as they begin to surround us. I immediately form a protective shield of smoke around us to prevent and slow down any further attacks. "Shoot them all! I do not think my energy can hold this any longer!"

"I have a better idea. Release it!"

"You sure?"

"Do it!" She demands.

I haltingly follow her demand, and as I let the smoke shield disperse, I watch as a bright ball of light, her energy, begins to swell between her hands. "WAIT, NO!" I exclaim when she flings the ball of energy to the ground beneath us.

I open my eyes to soaring barriers of light surrounding us, and Charlotte collapsed next to my feet. "CHARLOTTE!" I call out as the depth of the spell slowly and finally begins to diminish. "Why did you do that?!" I know she used if not all, most of her energy for that one! Bodies lay inert around us, so does the land, most of it scorched from the light. "Not now, Charlotte... I need you." I take up her body and retreat into the forest, where I set up a base. It is probably going to take a while for her energy to restore.

As I am sitting lying against the trunk of a tree with Charlotte resting her head on my thigh, I suddenly feel her move, attempting to lift her head. "Stay down, Charlotte. Your energy is still trying to restore." The sun is setting. I am sure we have so much more to get through.

'Why can't you just leave her, use the sword yourself, then come back for her?'

"I wish. We cannot fight against darkness with more darkness. Her powers are light." I am surprised he did not add an insult this time.

'Sure, you can fight darkness with darkness if you know what to do and how to do it.'

"I am not risking trying that. You are trying to get me killed. Any better plans that do not require me to do it myself?"

'Not that I know or can think of. But now that you have mentioned it, yes, I am trying to get you killed.'

"You must really loathe me."

'No, I just hate having to share a body with you.'

"It is my body!"

"Who are you talking to, Zane?" Charlotte asks, her voice sounding weary as if she just opened her eyes. Or maybe I woke her up.

"My shadow side," I answer. "I am sorry. Did I wake you?"

"No."

"How much did you hear?"

"All of it." She answers before sitting up.

"How do you feel?"

"Still a bit tired, but I think I will be able to pull through."

It has been hours, and we are not sure what is out there waiting for us now that we have revealed ourselves, but we have to finish this mission. I help her up, and we set off into the darkness.

In this mysterious castle-like structure, it appears small from the outer shell, but inside of it, everything is underground. Everybody seems to have their heads low, and in a rush. Not one person notices us intruding. Likely because of the attack we carried out earlier, and they are still trying to find who destroyed the land outside and injured and killed nearly every person who was out there at the time. We proceed further down into the dungeon chambers, trying to fit Philantha's last physical description to every person that passes us.

'Found her. She knows you are here.' He says.

"Where is she?"

'Behind you.'

I turn around, but there is no physical body in front of me.

'Look up.'

In the form of a damn bird, hovering and fluttering just above us. "There she is!" I call out as the little bird soars away from us. We immediately fly after it. She never thought I would find out about her and chase after her for cursing me all those years ago. "PHILANTHA!" She flies into an empty chamber with a large portcullis, and without second-guessing her motive, we follow. The portcullis falls behind us with a loud and shaking thud.

We both hear her loud cackles as she alters from a bird, back to human form. "What do you want, Prince Zane, and..." She glares, "Princess... Charlotte?"

"You know why we are here!"

"My memory is not as good as it used to be. Please clarify," She smirks. "Oh, right..."

"I want this curse undone, NOW! And if you will not do so, I can have you executed without a trial. Or I could just kill you with what you gave me."

"I could just kill you with what you gave me..." She mocks with a stupid and degrading voice, "I DO NOT CARE! YOU THINK THAT SCARES ME, YOU HAUGHTY BOY?! I have enjoyed watching you suffer all this time!"

"We do not want to fight you, let alone kill you, Philantha. Just undo the curse, and nobody will get hurt."

"What did Zane do to you?"

"He did not do anything, princess. I only cursed you to get back at your bitch of a grandmother and your mother. I knew you were going to run and tell your parents about me doing magic! They banned me from their kingdom just before you were born. I was not supposed to be there."

"What did they do to you?!"

"Oh, neither of them ever told you?" She snarls, "Your grandmother was the one who drove me, her own sister, out of our village when she discovered I was practicing voodoo. Even though she happened to be practicing shamanic magic herself and teaching your mother!"

"Look, I am sorry she —"

"SHUT IT, ROYAL BOY! I DO NOT WANT TO HEAR IT!"

A dark mass suddenly comes hurling toward me, that quickly knocks me back, then disperses before I could counter it. The chamber immediately goes quiet as I begin to feel something inside, a burning, like my organs are trying to wrench themselves from my body. My ears start to ring as inhumane shrieks torment them, and something attempts to force itself out of my body. And when it eventually snaps loose from me, and the shrieks finally come to a halt, I can see what that black mass created.

A clay coloured, distorted version of me, or what appears to be me, with black veins bulging from its skin and dark, empty sockets for eyes, twists its head towards me.

The mass did not create it; it is what has been talking to me degradingly all these years.

"Have fun, Zane!"

Charlotte and I immediately know who to go after individually, even though she possesses the power and the weapon to be able to weaken both of them. The distorted entity lets out another startling shriek at me before lunging for my neck, as Charlotte begins to use her more perilous magic against Philantha.

He grins viciously at me, tightening his grip on my throat. *'Hello, weaker side.'*

I am not sure how I am going to defeat him when we share the same powers. "STOP TALKING DOWN TO ME!" I snap, throwing him off guard by impelling the energy massed in my hand into him. "You are not stronger than me! You only think you are because I never fought back hard enough and allowed you to control me!"

He lets out a raucous, almost inhumane laugh, *'Stop opening your mouth and fight! Let's see if you really mean that.'*

I charge at him. My rage is forcing the energy I have left to amplify. Before I can take a firm grip on him, he disperses and continues to do so, the closer I attempt to get to catch him. He is trying to make me use all of my energy. Since he has now detached from me, if I run out of energy, that is it; I will collapse due to weakness.

'What is wrong? I thought you were stronger than me?'

Just as he wants, I begin to feel my energy drain, which causes me to collapse onto my knees. "I am..."

"ZANE!" I hear Charlotte call my name, just as I feel myself starting to lose sensibility. "HOLD ON!"

'You are NOT! I have not even punched you yet, and you are already giving in! You are weak, absolutely useless without me!'

My body is shutting down, but I forbearingly keep myself alert for a bit longer. Long enough to eventually feel the floor quake beneath me as Charlotte gives her all to her last attack. Light glistens through the cracks in the stone floor when she stomps her foot down. Finally drawing the enchanted sword out with her left hand, she slashes the gleaming blade across Philantha's throat—leaving the woman to bleed out until she stops breathing. When she eventually does stop breathing, her entire body contracts into a heap of black, ash appearing dust.

The only bad thing is now, my shadow side is still out of my body, and when he notices Charlotte with the sword that opposes his mischievous nature, he flees.

"Zane?" Charlotte rushes towards me after putting the sword back into its sheath.

My body finally gives in to the lack of energy.

⎯⎯⎯⎯⎯⎯⎯⎯⎯⎯ △ ⎯⎯⎯⎯⎯⎯⎯⎯⎯⎯

I awaken, back in my bedchamber, to a splitting headache.
"Damn..." I slowly sit up from beneath my covers to find Charlotte at
the end of the bed with her head down, fast asleep. "Charlotte?"

"Hm?"

"Thanks for having my back."

"You are welcome." She smiles warmly with her lips, keeping her
eyes closed, appearing as if she is half asleep. "We are not done yet."
She says before opening her eyes.

I hesitate. "What do you mean we are not done?"

"Whatever that shadow was that Philantha made come out of you. It
is still out there. I could not catch up to it."

Oh right, that. "It should not be hard to spot if we look for him."

"That is the problem, Zane. We do not know where he could have
gone. Looking for it will certainly take a while."

"True..." Hopefully, he is not a shapeshifter as well.

Chapitre 4

Sometime after Charlotte leaves, I find myself among confused people and my parents, claiming to have seen me awake and walking around already. That means it may still be here, walking around the castle. But if it has a distorted appearance, why are they not able to see it the way it appeared to Charlotte and me?

I go around the castle twice, trying to catch my shadow pretending to be me in his tracks, before leaving to get Charlotte. "Charlotte! I need you!"

"Did you find it?" She asks while securing the ribbon of her corset on the back of her dress.

"It is going around pretending to be me."

"What the hell!" She gasps, "That is frightening!"

"You are going to fight with a corset on?" I ask half questioningly when she runs to grab the sword.

"Shut up, Zane. It does not matter what I am wearing."

"Okay..." Feels weird without my shadow hurling all kinds of insults at me and calling Charlotte derogatory names for how she rightfully responds. By the time we arrive back to the castle, the confusion has arisen, even more, noticing the real me has returned after leaving earlier. So, we decide to split up and go around asking if they have seen me roaming around anywhere. Then I get around to my parents, whom both have seen and talked to my shadow shortly before Charlotte and I arrived. He is trying to replace me. "That was not me. I have not approached or talked to either of you all day. That was my shadow."

Almost immediately, like I am speaking a foreign language to them, they slowly turn their heads to look at each other before looking back at me, "What?"

"Mom, dad," I disclose calmly, "I was cursed when I was a kid, by Philantha. You remember her, she is dead, Charlotte and I killed her last night, or so we think we did. She cursed me with dark powers and a shadow that used to share my body with me, and never left me alone until she detached him from me. Now he is running around here pretending to be me and wants to kill me."

"Zane... are you okay?"

"Mom, I am fine. You can ask Char—"

"ZANE, I FOUND HIM!" I hear Charlotte suddenly shout.

"Excuse me," I mutter, before bolting out of the chamber in the form of smoke. And for the first time, in front of my parents. The likely reason he did not carry out trying to kill me while he still had an extended chance to last night was that he knew Charlotte was protecting me.

At least this time, we are a little more informed and know he will try to use that method he used on me; try to drain both of our powers. He proceeds to move all over the place as we chase after him. Hoping we would eventually get tired, and our energies would begin draining, but strangely no. At least not yet. However, we can somehow sense his energy starting to plummet, like a sudden seventh sense. He finally stops in the middle of the forest, some distance from my kingdom. "Tired?" I smirk. Now he knows how I felt.

"Her powers transferred," He asserts, "You both have Philantha's infinite energy! But that is fine... it will transfer back when I kill you both!"

Does that mean he was feeding off of her energy and is now weaker than us? "Then you are back to square one. You are weak!"

"I AM NOT!"

"And we are not fighting you; you are already weaker than us. You might as well give up." Charlotte smiles as a glowing ball of energy begins to expand between her hands. Hopefully, this one will not leave her drained and unresponsive like it did the first time.

He has a final plan in mind. Using the remainder of the energy he has left, he lunges at me, then dissipates before me. Not knowing what he has just done; all hell breaks loose inside of my body as I feel my organs start to burn once again. Charlotte drops her ball of energy when my eardrums instantly burst to something similar to an implosion, singeing my insides.

"Charlotte... Charlotte! I am okay!" I try to affirm as she is looking up at someone with tears flowing down her cheeks. She does not hear me, nor does she look down at me to imply so. "Charlotte!" She still does not look at me. "What are y—" I half ask before sitting up and passing right through her physical body. I cannot even feel the weight of my own. "What?" I whisper to myself before turning my head and noticing the reason why I cannot feel the weight of my clothes and armour. And why Charlotte does not notice me and cannot hear me. My soul has detached from my body. I am dead.

Blood seeps out of my body's ears, and a dark, smoke-like mist is discharging from it like a slowly diminishing fire. An invisible barrier prevents me from touching my body. I am not sure how to get back into it if I am blocked from doing so... if I ever will be able to have it back.

"I advise waiting until all of that darkness leaves his body before pronouncing him dead. It will take a while, but it should give clarity. Inform his kingdom." Agatha tells Charlotte. She does not appear or seem distressed about the possibility of me being dead like Charlotte is. I hope that means she is right about waiting for the darkness to leave my body.

I choose to follow Agatha with my body, only because I do not want to see the reaction of my parents or anybody when Charlotte tells them.

I feel awful. I know this is not my fault, but witnessing the devastation and distress on everybody's faces, trying to comprehend the possibility that I might not wake up. It is agonizing. I am sitting, watching the cloud of darkness continue to slowly leave my body and waiting for the shield preventing me from touching it to go away, possibly. I look up for the last time and notice three more people approach my body: Princess Maxine, Charlotte, and someone with a sterling crown and ash blonde hair. Prince Nathaniel! The curse finally broke, and he looks like himself again... but how?

I watch as Maxine leans in close to my face, whispers into my ear, then kisses my cheek.

If I wake, I am not going to let her know I saw her do that. I am glad to know she does not hate me anymore... and she has her best friend back. But Charlotte, she immediately breaks down, which makes my heart shatter. I know she gave herself powers to help me and let me know she was there for me, but I did not think she cared that much about me aside from that. She lets her tears fall onto my face as she weeps quietly before kissing my lips.

It shatters the barrier between my body and me, and the endless cloud of darkness finally ceases hovering over my body. "Can I...?" I ask as I extend my arm towards it. My hand passes through it. "Yes." Feeling and knowing I am back into my physical body; I calmly open my eyes. Making Maxine and Nathaniel jerk back in fear, but Charlotte at first does not notice. "Charlotte."

She looks up at me with her tear-filled, azure eyes, and I smile warmly at her. "ZANE!" She exclaims, charging forward for another kiss on the lips, and I eagerly requite it.

Acknowledgements

Christina, you started this, I finished it for you. I love you,
Rest In Peace.